I Am the King!

To Calou

Thanks to the hard work of C.N.L. for the realization of this story.
—N.D.

ISBN 0-439-37117-1

Copyright © 1999 by Nathalie Dieterlé. First American edition 2001 published by Orchard Books. First published in France in 1999 by Kaléidoscope under the title *C'est Moi le Roi!* All rights reserved. Published by Scholastic Inc. SCHOLASTIC and associated logos are trademarks and/or registered trademarks of Scholastic Inc.

12 11 10 9 8 7 6 5 4 3 2 1   1 2 3 4 5 6/0

Printed in the U.S.A.   24

First Scholastic paperback printing, November 2001

The text of this book is set in New Baskerville. The illustrations are gouache.

I Am the King!

Nathalie Dieterlé

SCHOLASTIC INC.

New York Toronto London Auckland Sydney
Mexico City New Delhi Hong Kong Buenos Aires

One day Little Louis's mom gave him a beautiful golden crown.

Little Louis proudly
went to check on
his subjects.

That night he fell asleep with his crown on.

The next day, King Louis decided to change all the laws of his kingdom.

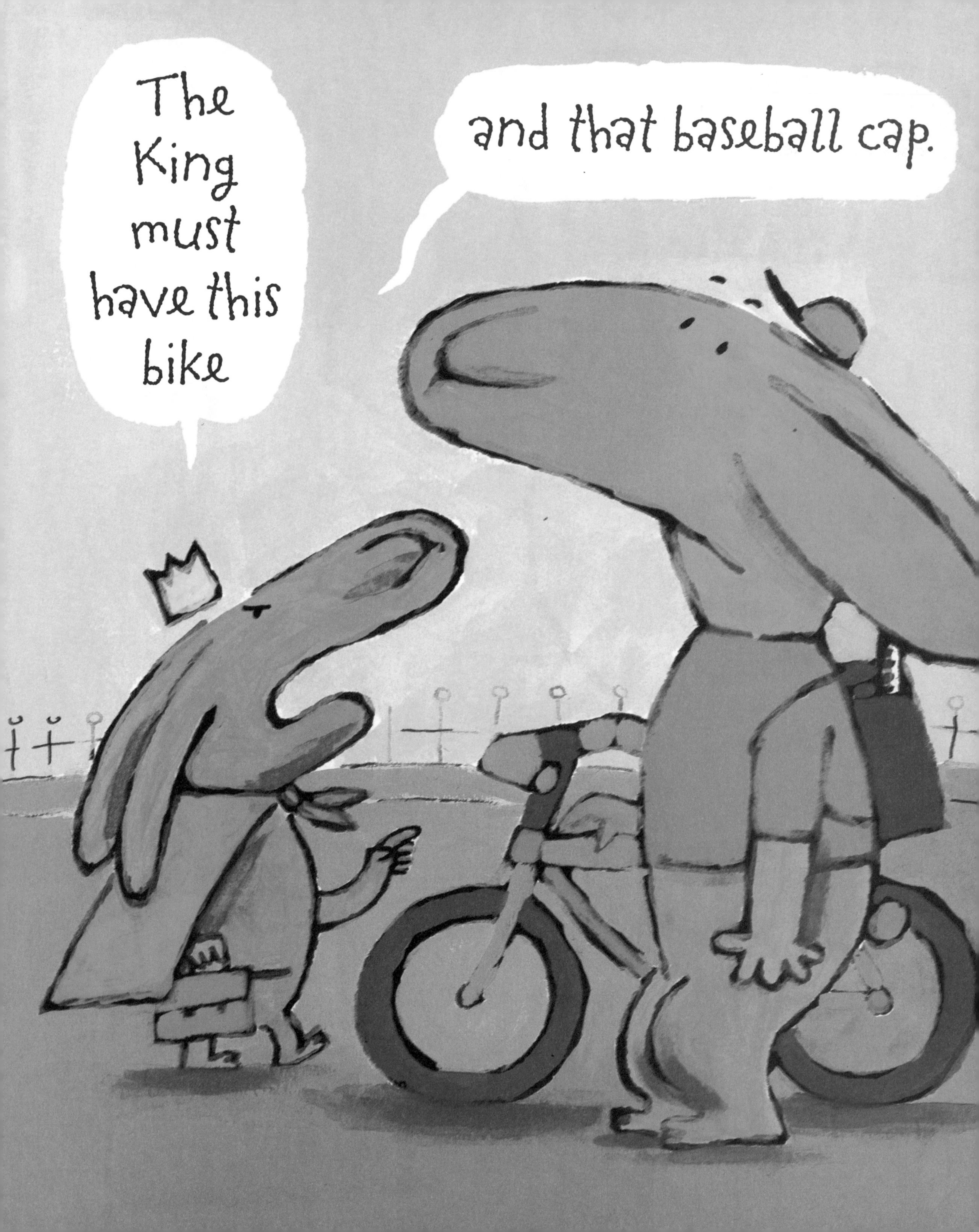
The King must have this bike
and that baseball cap.

"If that's the way it is, I won't be a king anymore," growled Little Louis.